artdecade monthly
2018 collection

artdecade monthly
2018
collection

selected works
from the galleries of
artdecademonthly.com

FURPLANET

published and distributed by
furplanet.com

adults only

artdecademonthly.com

6
He's gettin ready for round 2

CAL, I SWEAR TO GOD...
YOU BETTER PUT THAT GOD DAMN THING AWAY BEFORE I BREAK IT INTO A HUNDRED PIECES.
SORRY, JACK, GOTTA GET A PIC OF THAT MONSTER FOR POSTERITY'S SAKE.
BESIDES, THE LAST PIC GOT, LIKE, FIVE THOUSAND NOTES...

Willy's Daydream...

Happy B

Preve
Slips. Tri